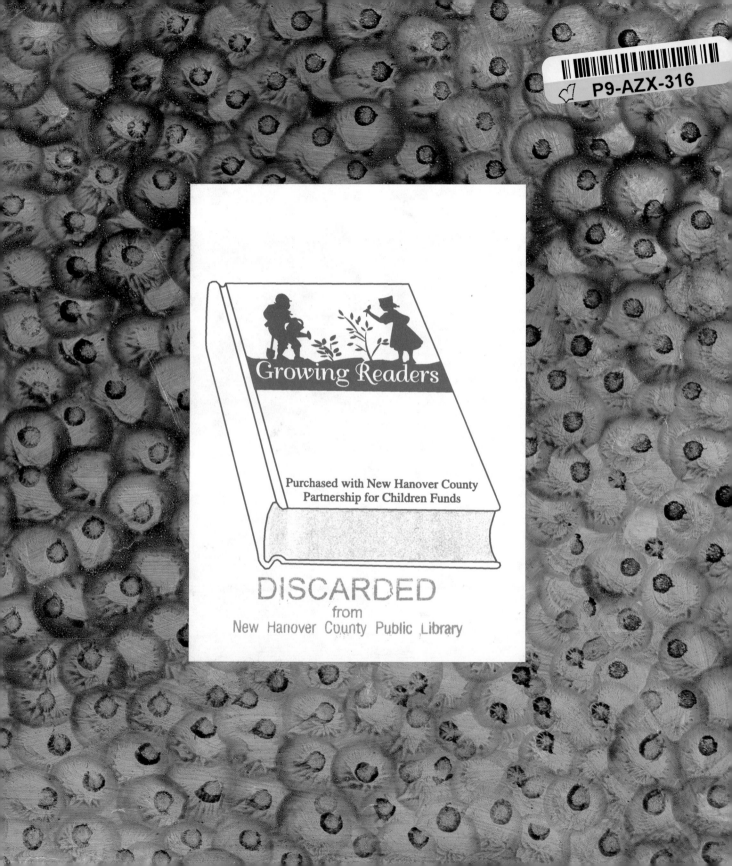

For Christopher F.

CIP Data is available.
Published in the United States 1997 by Dutton Children's Books,
a division of Penguin Books USA Inc.
375 Hudson Street, New York, New York 10014

Originally published in Great Britain 1996 by Andersen Press Ltd., London
Typography by Lilian Rosenstreich
Color separated in Switzerland by Photolitho AG, Zurich
Printed and bound in Italy by Grafiche AZ, Verona

First American Edition
ISBN 0-525-45757-7
2 4 6 8 10 9 7 5 3 1

TOAD

Ruth Brown

Dutton Children's Books • New York

This is the tale of a toad.

A muddy toad, a mucky toad,
a clammy, sticky, gooey toad,

odorous, oozing, foul and filthy,
and dripping with venomous fluid.

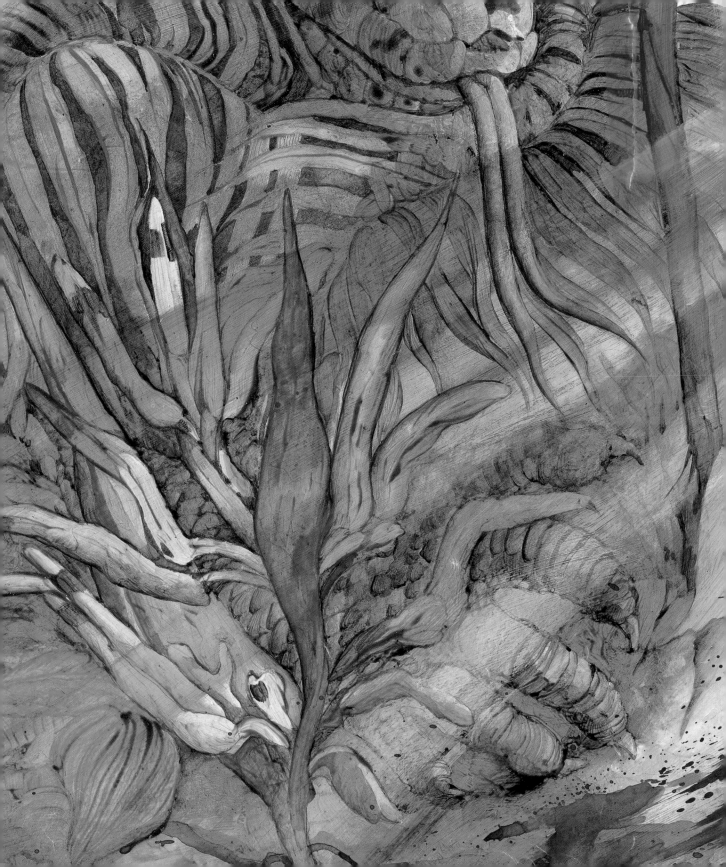

Toad's covered in warts and lumps
and bumps, with stains and
spots and speckled humps.

He's nasty, septic, toxic, and bitter,
and he leaves a slimy trail.

Toad is also a bug-crunching toad—
a greedy, fly-munching, worm-slurping toad.

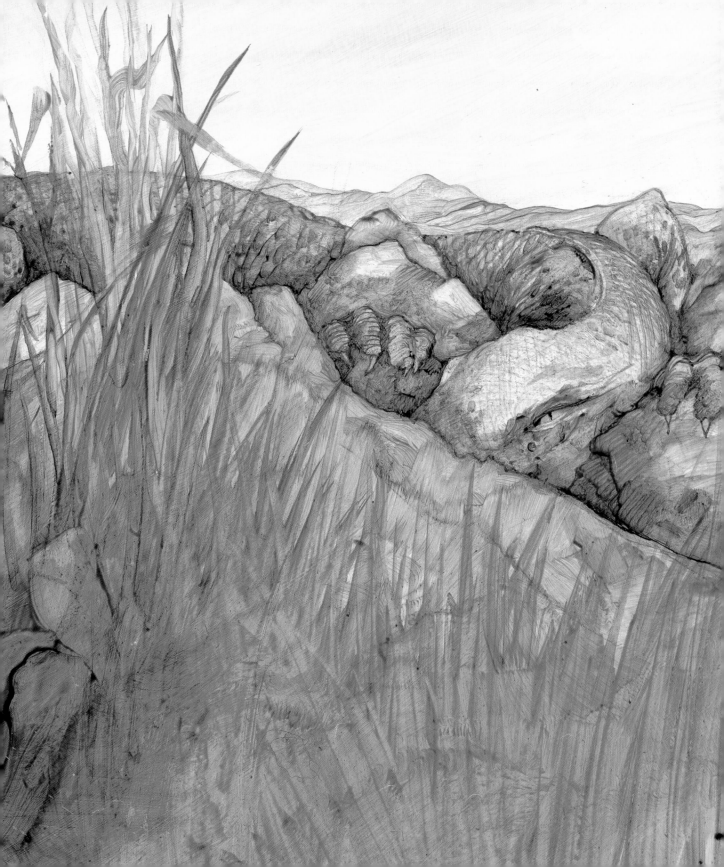

He is clumsy and careless, sluggish and slow,

and he can't even see very well.
So, winking and blinking,
he waddles and stumbles,
trudges and trundles

straight into the jaws of a monster!

Yuuuuuuck!

yells the monster.
It spits out the toad—

the happy toad, the safe toad,
the carefree and self-confident toad,

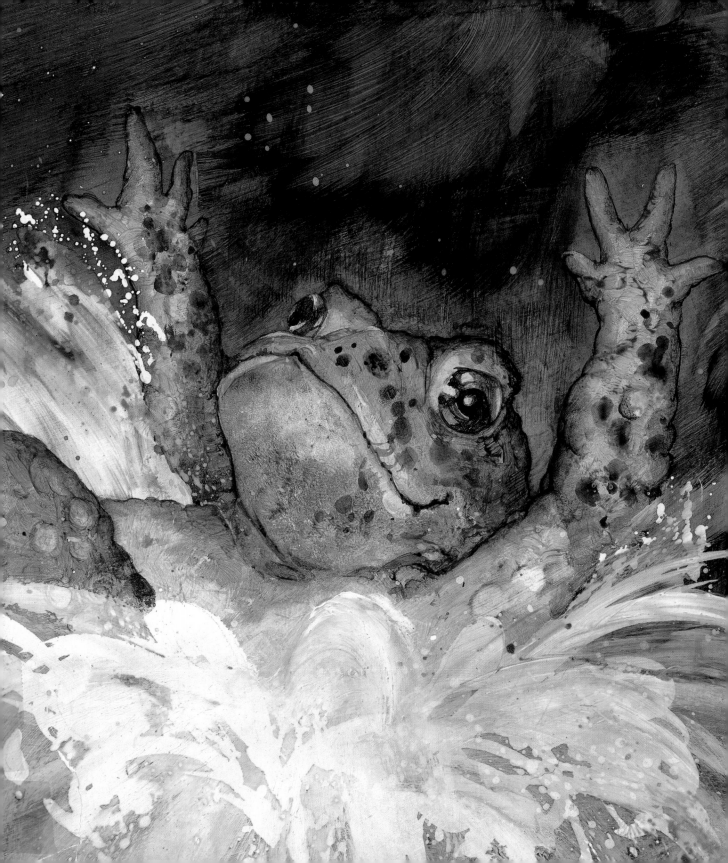

the toad with a monstrous smile.